This book belongs to

_____

ISBN: 978-168-859-070-0

Illustration by Amanda Blair

Layout: Jennifer Stolzer
www.jenniferstolzer.com

Adeline's Kindness

By Jennifer Stolzer
Illustrated by Amanda Blair

Adeline was a good girl
with an amazing Kindness.
She loved Kindness. When she
did things with Kindness
she always felt good.

Adeline did her
best to do everything
with Kindness and show
Kindness to others.

At home she would show
Kindness to her dog and cats.

At the park she would show
Kindness to the birds.

She would even show Kindness
to the bugs in the backyard when
she played in her sandbox.

Washing the dishes was
not on Adeline's chore list, but she
knew that helping her mother with
Kindness would make the dishes go
extra fast. Helping was fun, too.
It felt good to make her
mother happy.

"Thank you, Adeline," her mother said. "I'm so proud of you for helping when I asked." Her mother gave her a dollar for the ice cream stand.

Adeline was so happy
she danced out the door.

"Be back before dark!"
her mother called.

On the way to the ice
cream stand, Adeline found her
brother Jason on the curb.
He was crying.

"What's wrong?" Adeline asked.
"My skateboard broke," Jason replied.
Sure enough, he'd broken his
skateboard right in half.

Adeline hated to see her
brother so sad. She looked at
him with Kindness and knew
exactly what to do.

She took her dollar to
the ice cream stand.

Although she would have
liked the ice cream herself,
she gave the ice cream to her
brother with Kindness.

Adeline had to hurry home if she wanted to finish her sandcastle before dinner.

On the way, she showed Kindness to a turtle, her next door neighbor, and to nature by cleaning up litter she found

"Hello, Adeline," her mother said. "Wash your hands, it's time for dinner."

Adeline knew she wasn't
supposed to talk back to her mother,
but she couldn't help it and whined.
"I want to keep playing outside!"

"You can play outside tomorrow,"
her mother said in her serious voice.
"Wash your hands and set the table."

Adeline was quiet while her
family ate dinner. She asked to be
excused, took her plate to the sink,
and went upstairs to her room.

Adeline didn't know why she felt angry.
Being nice to people always made her happy,
and today she was nice to so many people!
But one thing went wrong and
she wasn't happy anymore.

Then, Kindness spoke.

"Adeline," Kindness said. "It is okay to be disappointed that you can't play outside. You are such a goodhearted girl, but even the most goodhearted people need kindness sometimes.

You have spent all day showing kindness to everyone around you. Now it's time to show kindness to yourself."

Adeline rested in Kindness's arms and forgave herself for being angry. She felt herself fill back up with love.

"You were kind to your
mom by helping, and you were
kind to your brother by sharing
your ice cream," Kindness said.
"What is something you can
do to be kind to yourself?"

"I can't build a sandcastle
until tomorrow," Adeline said.
"But maybe we can build a
block castle instead."

"That sounds like a good idea,"
Kindness said.

They spent the evening building blocks.
It was a nice thing Adeline could do for herself
and it helped her feel less tired and more happy.
"Remember to be kind to the world all around you,"
Kindness said. "But never forget to also
be kind to yourself."

The End

Author

Jennifer Stolzer is an author-illustrator from St. Louis, MO where she serves as secretary for the St. Louis Writers Guild. She is author of the Dog Park series for kids, and the Threadcaster series for all ages. She does her best to create bright, colorful characters both in words and pictures.

Illustrator

Amanda Blair grew up in southeastern Michigan. Beloved animated films and cartoons inspired her to begin drawing at a young age and she has continued improving it over the past fifteen years. She has a love for birds, art, and stories about family.

Made in the USA
Lexington, KY
08 September 2019